DINOSAUR COVE™

STALKING THE FANNED PREDATOR

Series created by
Working Partners Ltd

by
REX STONE

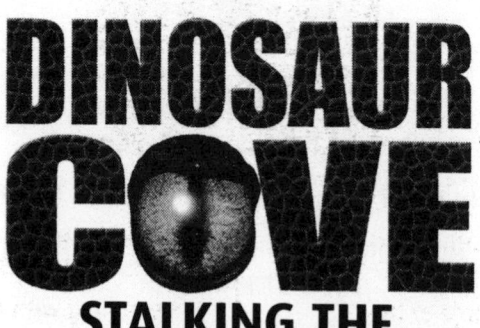

illustrated by
MIKE SPOOR

OXFORD
UNIVERSITY PRESS

D1392172

Special thanks to Jane Clarke

To my number one fossil hunter, Iona Churchill R.S.

My illustrations in this book are dedicated to
Elizabeth Alice M.S.

OXFORD
UNIVERSITY PRESS

Great Clarendon Street, Oxford OX2 6DP
Oxford University Press is a department of the University of Oxford.
It furthers the University's objective of excellence in research, scholarship,
and education by publishing worldwide in

Oxford   New York

Auckland Cape Town Dar es Salaam Hong Kong Karachi
Kuala Lumpur Madrid Melbourne Mexico City Nairobi
New Delhi Shanghai Taipei Toronto

With offices in

Argentina Austria Brazil Chile Czech Republic France Greece
Guatemala Hungary Italy Japan Poland Portugal Singapore
South Korea Switzerland Thailand Turkey Ukraine Vietnam

Oxford is a registered trade mark of Oxford University Press
in the UK and in certain other countries

British Library Cataloguing in Publication Data

Data available

ISBN: 978-0-19-275628-2

1 3 5 7 9 10 8 6 4 2

Printed in Great Britain
Paper used in the production of this book is a natural,
recyclable product made from wood grown in sustainable forests
The manufacturing process conforms to the environmental
regulations of the country of origin

STALKING THE FANNED PREDATOR

DINOSAUR COVE

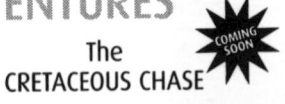

FACT FILE

➡️ JAMIE AND HIS BEST FRIEND, TOM, HAVE A SECRET—THEY'VE DISCOVERED A CAVE THAT LEADS THE WAY TO DINO WORLD! IF THE BOYS PLACE THEIR FEET INTO A SET OF FOSSILIZED DINOSAUR PRINTS, THEY'RE INSTANTLY TRANSPORTED TO AN ANCIENT LAND OF PREHISTORIC BEASTS. ONE DAY THEY GO ALL THE WAY BACK TO THE DEADLY PERMIAN ERA, AND FIND THAT THEY SOON NEED HELP FROM AN UNEXPECTED SOURCE…

JAMIE

- **FULL NAME:** JAMIE MORGAN
- **AGE:** 8 YEARS
- **SIZE:** 1 JATOM*
- **TOP SPEED:** 10 KPH
- **LIKES:** FOSSIL HUNTING AND LEARNING ABOUT DINOSAURS
- **DISLIKES:** BEING STUCK INDOORS

Jamie's eye

Jamie's foot

Jamie's hand

***NOTE:** A JATOM IS THE SIZE OF JAMIE OR TOM: 125 CM TALL AND 27 KG IN WEIGHT

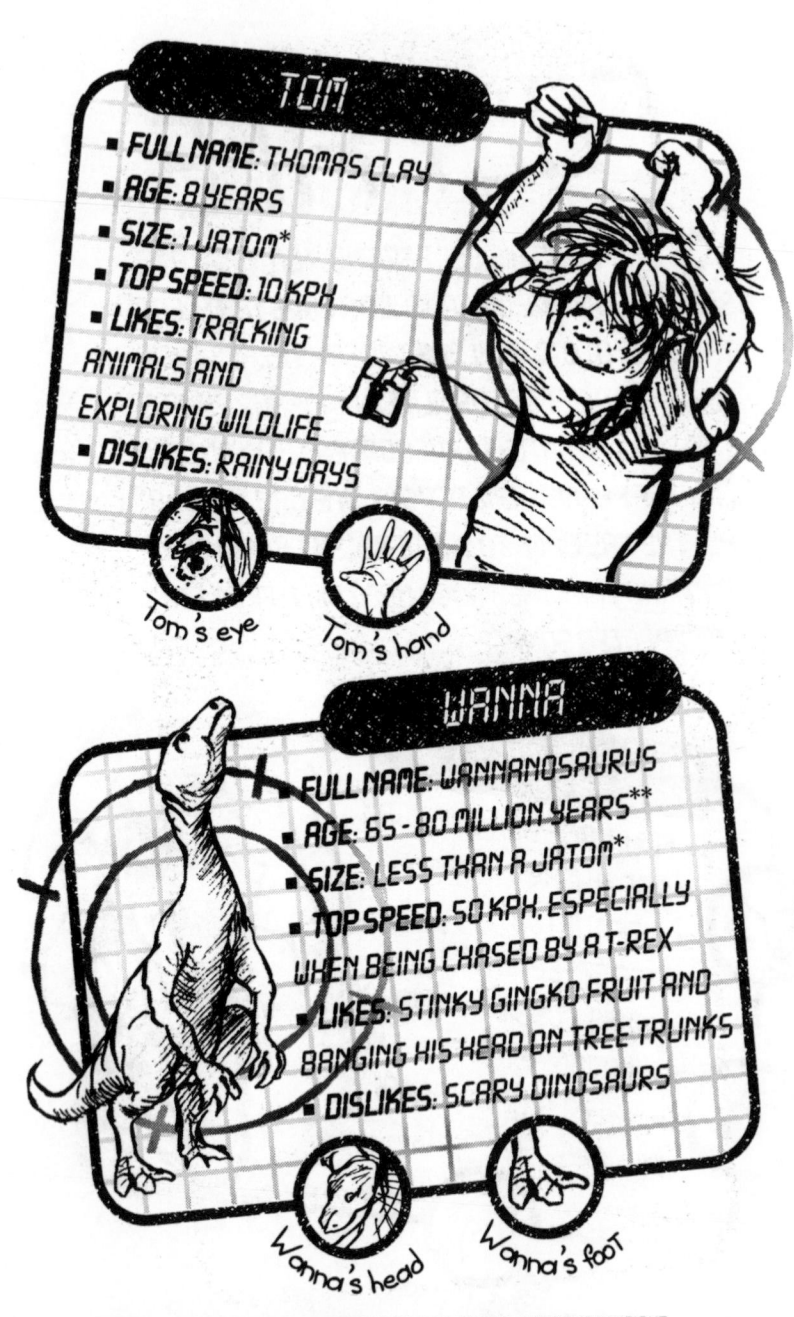

TOM

- **FULL NAME:** THOMAS CLAY
- **AGE:** 8 YEARS
- **SIZE:** 1 JATOM*
- **TOP SPEED:** 10 KPH
- **LIKES:** TRACKING ANIMALS AND EXPLORING WILDLIFE
- **DISLIKES:** RAINY DAYS

Tom's eye

Tom's hand

WANNA

- **FULL NAME:** WANNANOSAURUS
- **AGE:** 65 - 80 MILLION YEARS**
- **SIZE:** LESS THAN A JATOM*
- **TOP SPEED:** 50 KPH, ESPECIALLY WHEN BEING CHASED BY A T-REX
- **LIKES:** STINKY GINGKO FRUIT AND BANGING HIS HEAD ON TREE TRUNKS
- **DISLIKES:** SCARY DINOSAURS

Wanna's head

Wanna's foot

*NOTE: A JATOM IS THE SIZE OF JAMIE OR TOM: 125 CM TALL AND 27 KG IN WEIGHT
**NOTE: SCIENTISTS CALL THIS PERIOD THE LATE CRETACEOUS

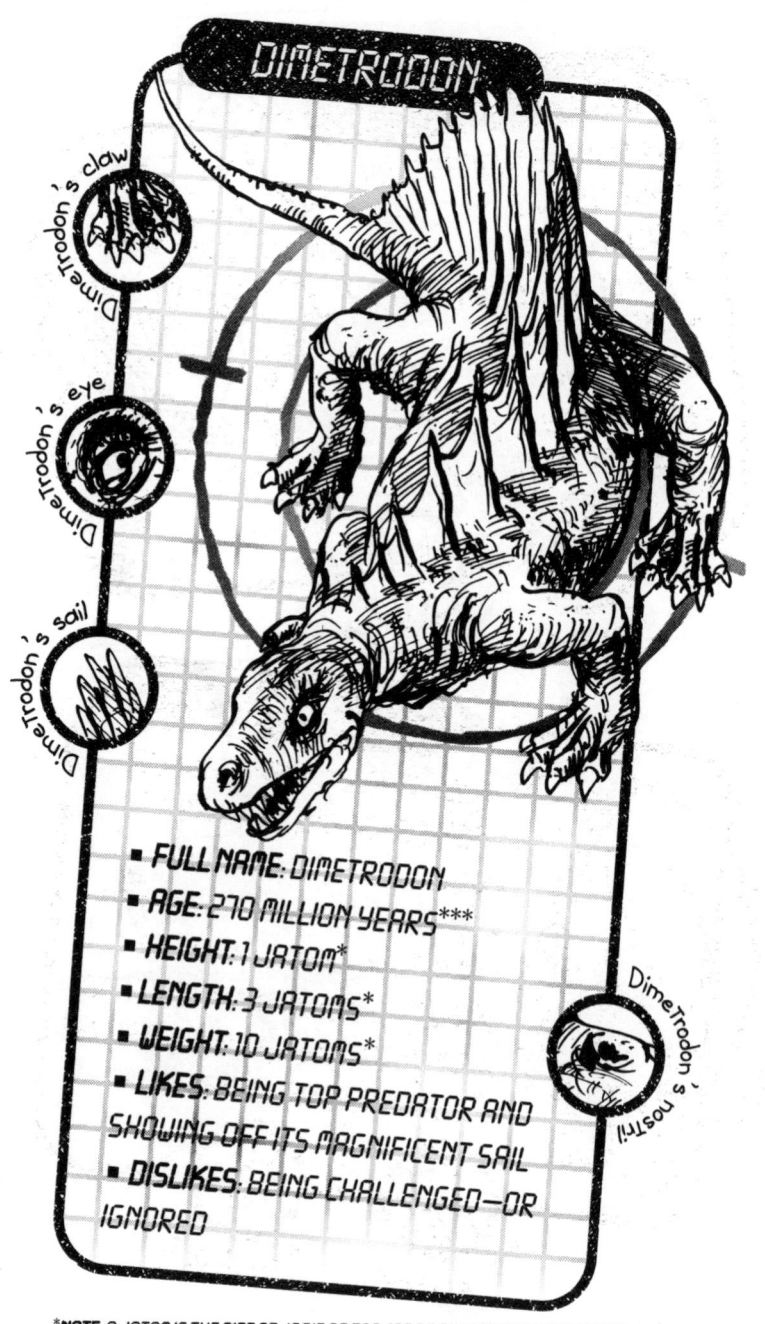

DIMETRODON

Dimetrodon's claw

Dimetrodon's eye

Dimetrodon's sail

Dimetrodon's nostril

- **FULL NAME:** DIMETRODON
- **AGE:** 270 MILLION YEARS***
- **HEIGHT:** 1 JATOM*
- **LENGTH:** 3 JATOMS*
- **WEIGHT:** 10 JATOMS*
- **LIKES:** BEING TOP PREDATOR AND SHOWING OFF ITS MAGNIFICENT SAIL
- **DISLIKES:** BEING CHALLENGED—OR IGNORED

*NOTE: A JATOM IS THE SIZE OF JAMIE OR TOM: 125 CM TALL AND 27 KG IN WEIGHT
***NOTE: SCIENTISTS CALL THIS PERIOD THE PERMIAN

DINOSAUR COVE

Village

Marina

Sealight Head

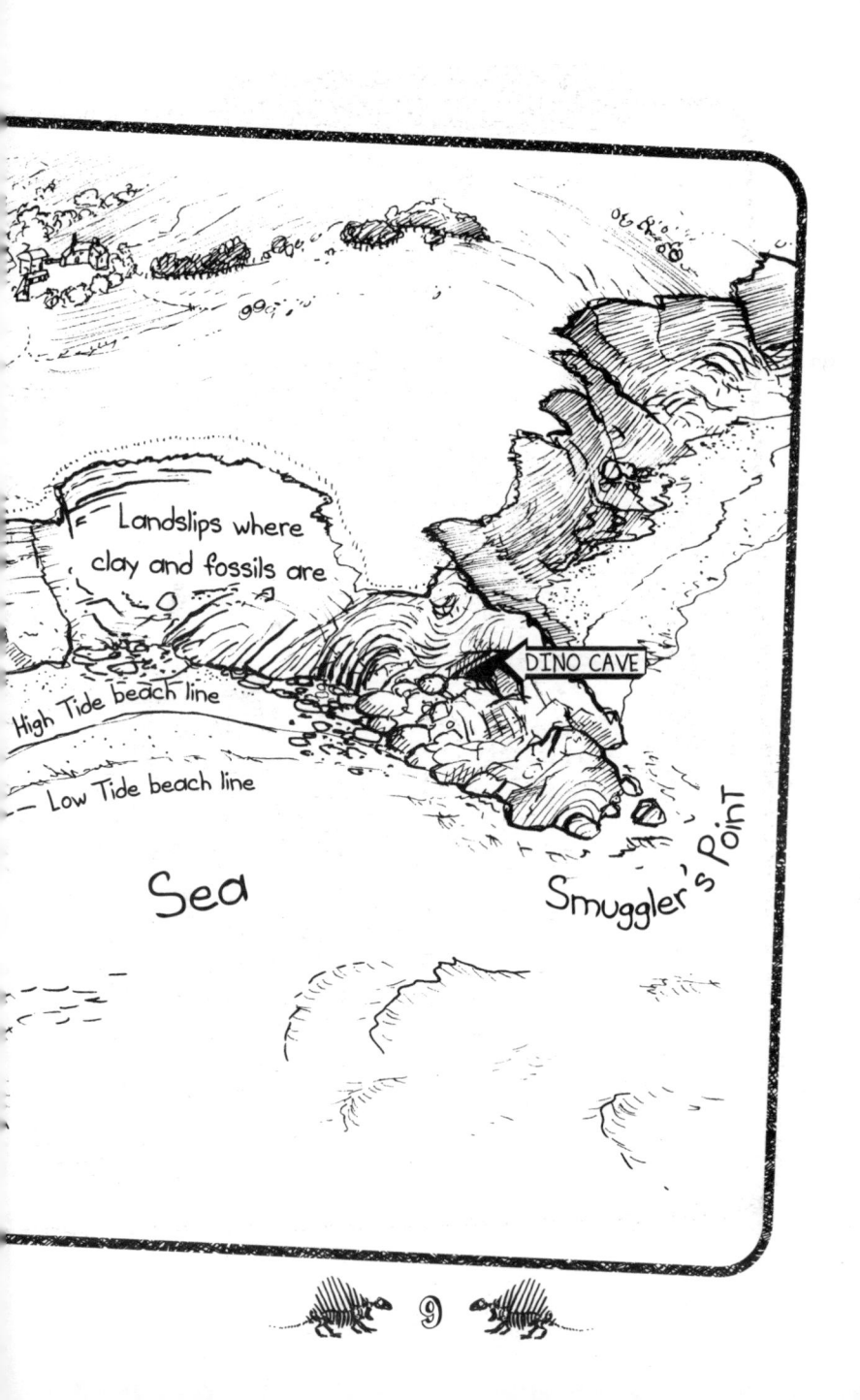

Landslips where clay and fossils are

DINO CAVE

High Tide beach line

Low Tide beach line

Sea

Smuggler's Point

9

CHAPTER 1

SEARCH:

'Check this out. It looks like a giant stone woodlouse!' Jamie Morgan told his best friend Tom Clay, pointing to a hand-sized fossil on the display table. The weird fossil creature had a rounded head with big bug eyes and a body divided lengthwise into three ridges.

'That'd give your grandad a scare if he found it in the woodpile.' Tom laughed.

'It didn't live on land, you wombat,' Jamie said with a grin. 'It's a trilobite. They were sea creatures, like ammonites.'

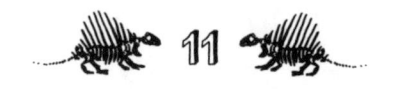

It was Fossil Finders' Day at Jamie's dad's dinosaur museum in Dinosaur Cove. Jamie and Tom had spent all morning putting out the trestle tables and hanging up the strings of brightly coloured flags that were now fluttering in the sunshine. Fossil hunters from all over had come to show their finds and take part in the Best Fossil competition.

'This one's curled up into a ball.' Tom was looking at a deck-of-cards-sized fossil trilobite. 'Cool! I reckon it's better than the woodlouse one.'

Jamie picked up a tiny trilobite the size of his finger nail with eyes that looked like miniature honeycombs. 'Naw, this one should win the blue rosette!' he exclaimed. 'Even though it's tiny, I can make out all the ridges along its back.'

A woman with a ponytail walked over to them. 'That's my trilobite,' she said proudly. She raised her voice. 'It's a much finer, more detailed, specimen than the other two, isn't it?' she said, glancing mischievously at two men standing beside the table.

'That's what *you* think,' the first man spluttered, peering over the top of his glasses and picking up his woodlouse-like fossil. 'I think *my* fossil is the best.'

'No, no, no, mine is vastly superior,' the second man chuckled into his beard. 'But it's for the judge to decide.'

'The judge is my dad,' Jamie told them. 'Here he comes now. Hey, Dad,' he called, 'why don't we have any of these cool trilobites in our museum?'

'Because our museum's a dinosaur museum,' Mr Morgan

explained, 'and there weren't any trilobites around by the time of the dinos. They'd all died out in a mass extinction at the end of the Permian Era.' Mr Morgan paused, with a dreamy look on his face. 'Now, that was a fascinating time period . . . '

Jamie glanced at Tom and raised his eyebrows. No one else knew it, but they had discovered a secret cave which led back to the prehistoric world. They'd come face to face with awesome creatures in the age of the dinosaurs and the Ice Age. But they'd never gone back to a time before dinos!

'Cool!' Tom said. He looked meaningfully at Jamie. 'So did any *big* creatures live in the Permian?' he asked.

'Loads!' Jamie's dad said. 'They were the ancestors of mammals and dinosaurs. Dimetrodon, for example . . . '

'I have a poster of dimetrodon.' The woman with the ponytail reached beneath the table and unrolled a picture of the fossil skeleton of a humongous clawed lizard with sharp teeth and a tall fan of spines along its back.

'Awesome!' Tom exclaimed.

'What were the spines for?' asked Jamie.

'They supported a sail,' the woman told him. 'Dimetrodon lived in a desert that was freezing cold at night and

DIMETRODON

burning hot in the day, so the sail helped it heat up and cool down . . . '

'No, no, no,' the man with the beard interrupted her. 'The sail was like a peacock's tail. The creature used it to impress a mate.'

'You're both wrong,' said the man in the glasses. 'The sail made it look bigger. Dimetrodon used it to scare off predators.'

The woman laughed. 'Experts hardly ever agree,' she said. 'Who do you think is right?' she asked the boys.

'Hard to say,' Tom said slowly, fingering the binoculars around his neck. 'We'll have to look into it, won't we, Jamie?'

'Right!' Jamie nodded. He knew what Tom was thinking. To find a real live dimetrodon, they'd need to take a Permian fossil with them to bring them out in the right time period.

'Please may we borrow a trilobite fossil?' he asked politely.

'To help us with our research,' Tom chipped in.

'Will this do?' The woman rummaged under the table and gave Jamie a tissue-wrapped stone that fitted into the palm of his hand.

Jamie unwrapped the trilobite. Two goggly stone eyes looked up at him.

'Perfect!' he said, putting it carefully into his pocket. 'Thanks. We'll bring it back soon.'

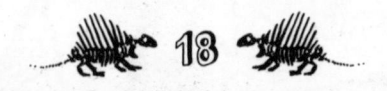

'Time I got on with the judging.' Jamie's
dad picked up his clipboard. 'Have fun
researching the Permian!' he told the boys.

Jamie and Tom dashed into the lighthouse,
grabbed Jamie's backpack and rushed to
the smugglers' cave on the headland above
Dinosaur Cove. Jamie's heart beat faster

as they squeezed through
the gap into the secret cave
and fitted their feet into the line of fossil
dinosaur footprints that led across the stone
floor of the cave. They counted the steps,
'One,

two,

three,

four...

five!'

There was a blinding flash of light.
Then everything went dark.

'Are we still in the cave?' Jamie
wondered aloud. He couldn't see a
thing. He felt the trilobite in
his pocket.

'Why didn't it
work?' Tom
whispered.

CHAPTER 2

'I don't know what's going on,' Jamie said.

Gradually, Jamie's eyes adjusted to the darkness. There was a faint light ahead, so he and Tom edged towards it. Their feet made scrunching noises on the ground.

'We're walking on sand, not rock . . . ' Tom murmured. 'So we can't be in the cave in Dino Cove.'

Grunk!

The noise came from above them.

Grunk, grunk, grunk!

'Wanna!' Tom and Jamie exclaimed together, looking up. Their dinosaur friend's bony head was poking through a narrow tunnel up through the rocks, surrounded by a halo of dry ferns.

'The trilobite worked,' Jamie said excitedly. 'We've come out in a new cave in the Permian Era.' He squeezed into the narrow gap in the rocks and began to haul himself up it. The air

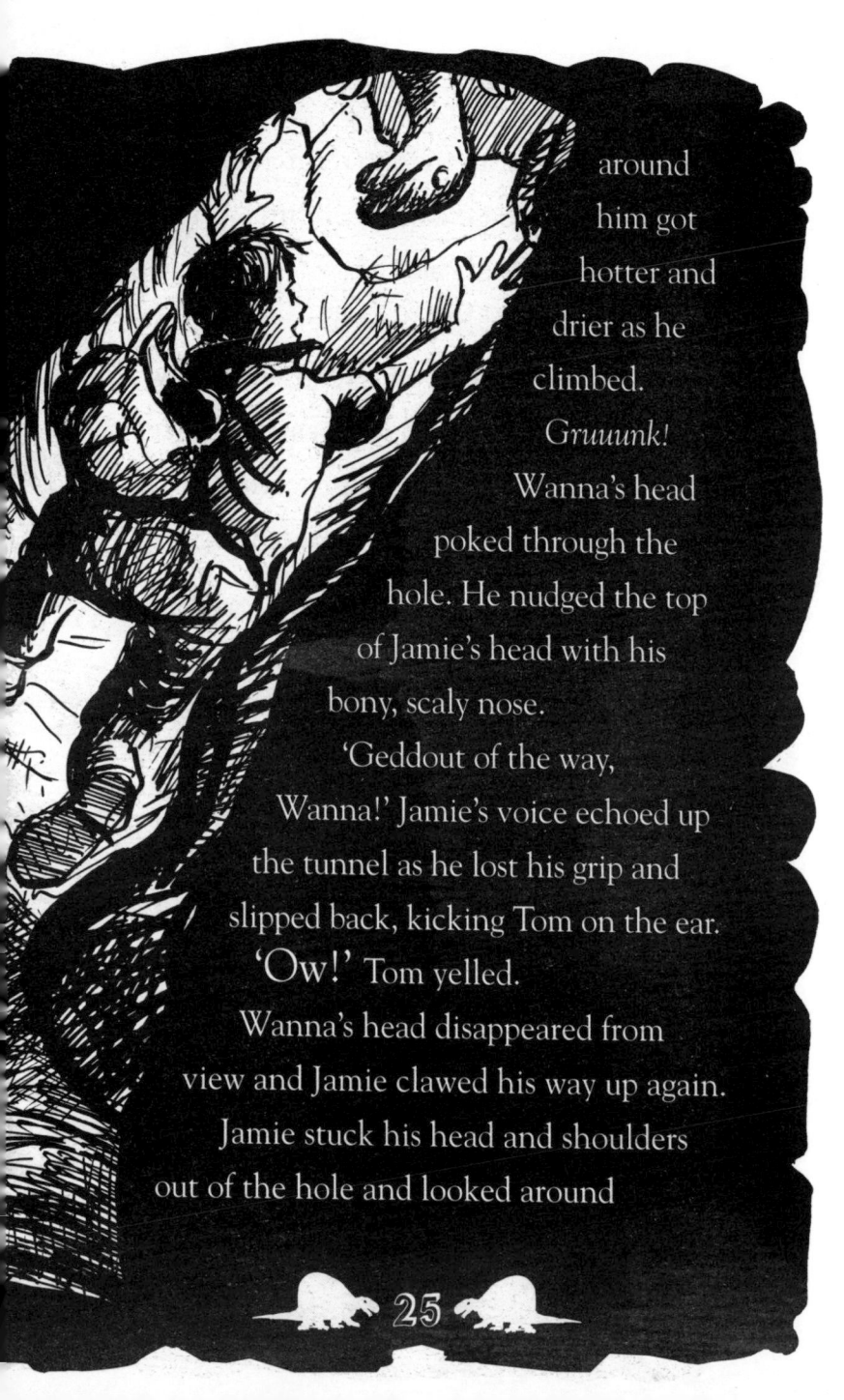

around him got hotter and drier as he climbed.

Gruuunk!

Wanna's head poked through the hole. He nudged the top of Jamie's head with his bony, scaly nose.

'Geddout of the way, Wanna!' Jamie's voice echoed up the tunnel as he lost his grip and slipped back, kicking Tom on the ear.

'Ow!' Tom yelled.

Wanna's head disappeared from view and Jamie clawed his way up again. Jamie stuck his head and shoulders out of the hole and looked around

cautiously. The entrance to their
cave was at the base of a mountain.
Aside from the ferns and a few
stunted cycads, all he could see were
dusty red rocks and a vast expanse of gritty
red desert sand. The sun was beating down
and the air tasted dry and dusty. The dead
ferns rustled. He felt a long lizardy tongue
wriggle into his ear.

Sluuurp!

'Yuck!' Jamie shrieked, shaking off the
dino drool. 'You're not helping, Wanna.'
He scrambled out of the hole and reached
down a hand to help haul Tom out.

'It's good to see you, again, too, Wanna.'
Tom laughed as Wanna raced round and
round them, grunking happily and wagging
his scaly tail.

'Now, where would a dimetrodon hang
out?' Jamie asked.

'Let's check out the view,' Tom suggested.
He began to scrunch up the crumbly
mountainside.

'It's hard to breathe,' Jamie wheezed
as Tom kicked up a cloud of red dust.

'I reckon there was less oxygen in
the Permian, just like there was in
the Triassic,' Tom puffed. 'It's just
like the atmosphere on top of a
high mountain.'

Wanna sneezed.

Phhht!

'Wannanosauruses don't belong
in the Permian,' Jamie remarked.
'There weren't any dinosaurs around then.'

27

'There's one around now,' Tom grinned. 'So that must make Wanna the very first dino ever!'

Grunk!

Wanna seemed to understand they were talking about him.

'Dinosaurs came along millions of years after the Permian ended.' Jamie was breathing easier now in the hot dry air. 'I read about it in one of Dad's books,' he said. 'The Permian Event was one of the worst mass extinctions

ever! Some scientists think more than ninety per cent of all creatures were wiped out.'

'What caused *that*?' Tom asked.

'They reckon loads of volcanic eruptions sent ash and poisonous gasses into the air and blotted out the sun,' Jamie said, clambering onto a huge flat rock. 'I just hope it's not today!' He shaded his eyes with his hand and gazed out across the desert as Tom and Wanna scrabbled up beside him.

'I can see the sea in the distance,' Jamie said, 'and a couple of places where it's green.'

Tom scanned the landscape with his binoculars. 'That's a conifer forest,' he said, pointing. He swung round. 'And that's a swamp with some strange trees growing around it . . .'

'Any sign of Permian beasties?' Jamie asked.

'Oh, wow!' Tom declared. 'Over there, in the desert. It's a group of dimeys. Take a look behind that big sand dune,' he said, handing the binoculars to Jamie.

It took a moment for Jamie to find them. The dimetrodons were deep red with burnt orange markings, and they blended into the desert as if they were wearing camouflage. Their legs sprawled out to the sides,

like monster lizards. They were too far away
to make out much detail, but it was easy to
identify them by their sails.

'Let's get closer.' Jamie skidded down the
dusty mountain on his heels, closely followed
by Tom and Wanna. They landed, spluttering
and coughing, in a patch of broad-leaf ferns.

'We can use these to keep us cool,' Tom
declared, picking up a couple of broken-off
leaves the size of skateboards.

Jamie took a big swig out of his water
bottle and handed it to Tom. Tom gulped the

water down thankfully, then sprinkled
a few drops on Wanna's head.

Gak, gak, gak!

Wanna shook his head in surprise.

'Thanks for the shower, Wanna,' Jamie
laughed.

They held the gigantic leaves over their
heads for shade as they trekked across the
baking red grit and slogged up the steep sand
dune they had seen from the viewpoint.

'Shhh!' Tom warned as they drew
closer. 'We don't want the dimeys
to hear us. They're meat eaters.'

The boys and Wanna
dropped to their stomachs
and peered over the
brow of the dune.
Ahead of them,
was a group of
five dimeys,

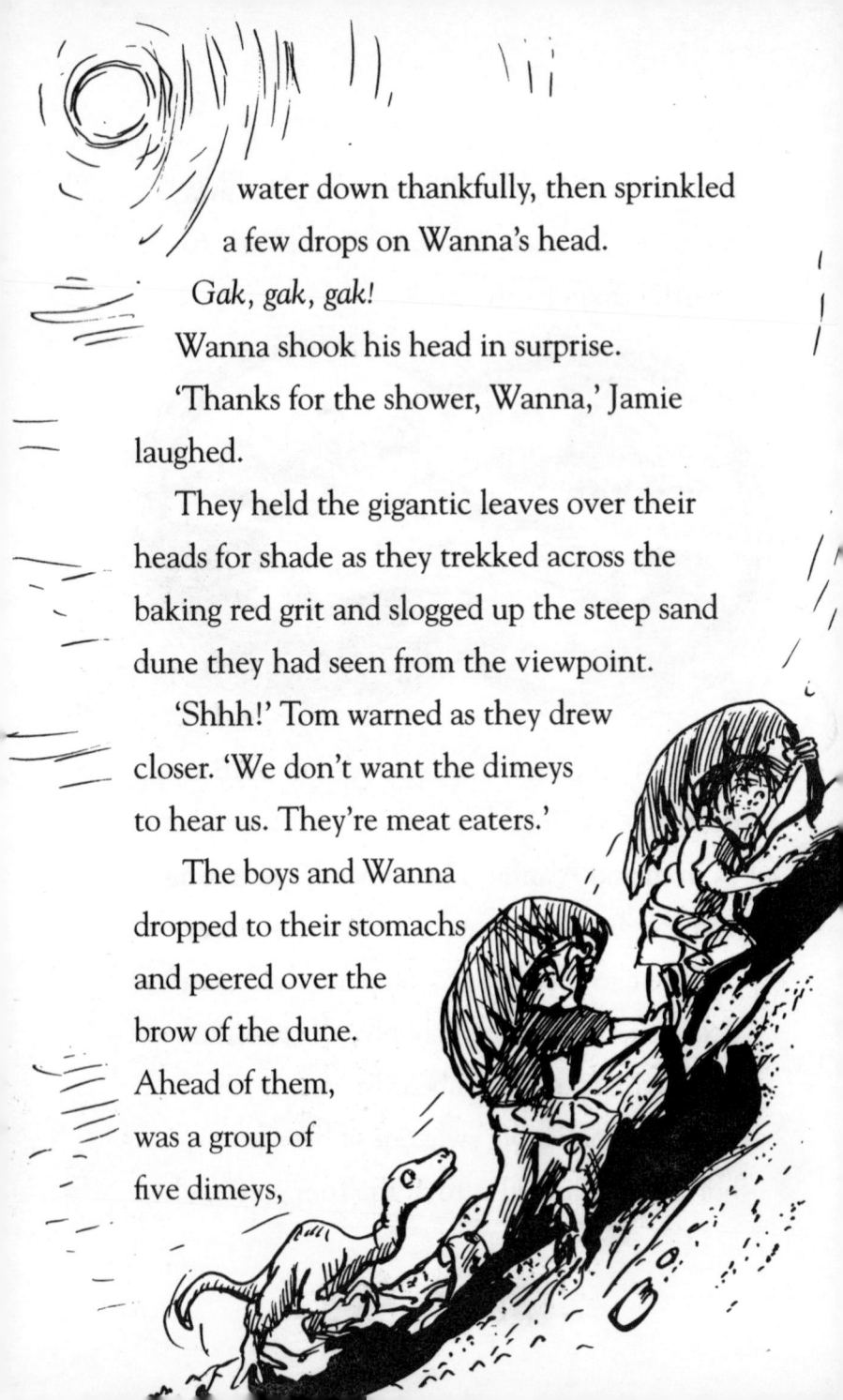

varying in size from a small one the size of a car wheel to one that was as big as a jeep.

'They've all put their sails down!' Tom whispered, pointing to the loose folds of scaly skin that lay along the dimetrodons' backs.

The dimeys were feeding on something, ripping into its flesh with the fearsome teeth in their long crocodile-like jaws.

'Phewey!' Jamie gagged. 'Their dinner stinks.'

'It's not a fresh kill,' Tom said in a low voice. 'They've found an old carcass.'

A sudden gust of wind blew across the desert.

'Feels good,' Jamie said as the breeze cooled his sweaty skin.

Below them, the dimeys stopped eating and turned their sides to the wind. Then they spread out the spines of their sails into huge crescent-shaped fans.

'Awesome,' Jamie commented.

As the boys watched, the dimeys stretched out their stumpy necks.

Urrr, they grunted, with their mouths gaping, *urr, urr, urr*.

'That's a prehistoric purr!' Tom murmured.

'So the lady was right; dimetrodons use their sails for cooling,' Jamie whispered, getting to his feet. 'I guess we should go back now and return her trilobite,' he said reluctantly.

There was a gust of wind behind them.

The dimeys stopped purring and turned to look up, mouths still agape. Drool began to drip from their fangs.

'Uh-oh. The wind has changed direction,' Tom warned. 'They've caught our scent.'

CHAPTER 3

The monstrous lizards hurled themselves
at the sand dune, hissing ferociously and
scrambling over each other in their effort to
get at the boys and Wanna. Wanna took one
look and turned tail, hurtling back down the
dune the way they had come.

The boys ran after him, but the dimeys
were catching up.

'I know!' Jamie shouted. 'We can dune
surf.' Jamie threw down his fern leaf and
jumped on. Tom did the same.

They whizzed down the dune, leaving
S-shaped trails and spraying sand all
over Wanna as they passed him.
At the bottom of the dune,
they leapt off the ferns and
looked back.

'No sign of the
dimeys,' Jamie declared. 'They've
given up the chase and gone back to their
smelly dinner.'

Wanna was still skittering down the dune
on his hind legs, picking up speed. Tom and
Jamie watched as he tripped over his big feet
and somersaulted over and over, landing with a
whump! on his bony skull. He jumped to his feet
and bounded off as if nothing had happened.

'Must be great having an inbuilt crash
helmet,' Jamie grinned.

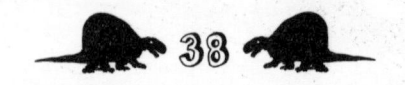

The boys left their
sand-blasted fern leaves
behind and scrunched after
Wanna, who was heading towards the
mountain. From here, they could see it
was cone-shaped and it had a flat
top with ragged edges.

'It's a volcano that's blown its top,' Jamie
murmured. 'Cool!'

Near the bottom of the volcano, low
ferny bushes sprouted between heaps of red
boulders. Some of the boulders were as big
as a bus. Wanna stopped beside a flat rock
and bobbed his head up and down, grunking
nervously.

'Dimey footprints!' Tom exclaimed. A track of dusty prints, each with five long claws, led across the flat rock. 'Wanna's warning us to watch out,' he whispered.

They edged round a giant boulder.

'Clever Wanna.' Tom gave him a pat.

Jamie cautiously looked round the edge of the boulder. There was a pair of adult dimetrodons right in front of them. This time, the huge lizard-like creatures were splotched with the same shades of reds and greens as the boulders and the ferns. The smaller dimey's sail lay flat along its back, but the larger of the two had its sail held high.

'What are they doing?' Jamie whispered.

'Not sure,' Tom admitted. 'We need a safe place to find out.'

'Up here!' Jamie shinned up the boulder, closely followed by Tom. They hauled Wanna up after them and lay flat, watching.

The larger of the two dimeys was strutting stiff-legged around the smaller dimey, raising and lowering its sail.

Geeeooow! Geeeooow! Geeeooow!

'It's a male showing off to a female,' Tom said.

The smaller dimey lay down with a sigh and closed her eyes.

'She's not interested,' Jamie chuckled.

But as he spoke, an even bigger dimey came swaggering out from behind a boulder.

'Look at that humongous sail,' Tom said. 'It's awesome.'

The smaller male dimey who had been there

first puffed out his sail as the female opened her eyes and leapt to her feet.

'And here,' Tom said, speaking quietly in his wildlife commentator's voice, 'we have two male dimetrodons competing for the attention of the female. The males are pulling out all their tricks. Just look at their sails furling and unfurling as they strut up and down in front of her. You can tell the female is impressed. Her eyes are fixed on the male with the biggest sail. She's moving towards him . . .'

Geeeooow!
Geeeooow!
Geeeooow!

GEE OW-OW-OW!

The screech came from the smaller male dimey as it stepped in front of the larger one.

'He doesn't want to lose his girlfriend!' Jamie said.

The two male dimeys spread out their sails and turned to face each other. The markings on their skin flushed crimson and bright green.

'They can change colours like chameleons,' Tom breathed. 'Wow!'

Quick as a flash, the two male dimetrodons lowered their sails and raised them again. Jamie was so close he could hear their spines rattling.

The dimeys' jaws gaped, and they stamped their feet.

'Now,' said Tom, speaking into his pretend microphone, 'we're about to be the first people—and dinosaur—in the world to witness a real live dimey fight!'

The two male dimeys roared towards each other, shrieking and snapping their toothy jaws. They barged shoulders with a bone-shaking *thunk!*

'They're trying to tip the other over,' Jamie said. 'They want to get a bite at the soft underbelly . . . '

'I don't think they're trying to kill each other,' Tom whispered. 'It's a show of strength. The bigger one's much stronger. Look. He's pushing the smaller one back.'

'The smaller one knows it,' Jamie said. 'He's putting his sail down . . . oh . . . he's giving up already.'

The winner proudly spread out its colourful sail and strutted around the female, uttering triumphant *geee-ow* noises.

'He *is* like a peacock,' Tom chuckled.

Ur . . . urrr.

The female dimey purred as she walked away with the victor.

Ow, ow, ow.

The male left behind whimpered,

and his bright colours faded to match the landscape once more.

Wanna grunked sympathetically.

'The small male was smart to keep out of trouble,' Tom declared. 'This way, he lives to fight and win a mate another day.'

'So the man with the beard was right, too,' Jamie remarked, as they continued on their way. 'He told us dimetrodons used their sails to attract a mate.'

'The man with the glasses said dimeys' sails made them look bigger to scare off predators,' Tom said thoughtfully. 'Could that be a third use?'

geee-ow

Grunk, grunk!

Wanna grunked insistently.

'What's up with Wanna?' Jamie wondered. Their dinosaur friend had stopped by a patch of ferns and was bobbing his head up and down. As the boys watched, he stuck his nose into a hole in the ground. Muffled grunking noises echoed around them.

'He's found the entrance to our cave,' Tom said.

'But we can't go back yet,' Jamie said. 'If we leave now, we'll never know if dimeys used their sails for protection.'

'Maybe there are more dimeys nearby?' Tom scanned the sides of the extinct volcano with his binoculars. 'Over there!' he exclaimed, pointing. 'There's a group in front of that cave.' He handed the binoculars to Jamie.

Around ten dimeys were gathered
on a platform in front of a cave in the
mountainside. Their sails were down and
they were feasting on the remains of another
carcass. Every so often they sniffed the air and
glanced over their shoulders.

'They can sense something else is about,'
Jamie said. 'But it can't be us. We're
downwind from them.'

'It might be another predator,' Tom warned.

'Let's circle up around the cave. They
won't attack us if we keep our distance.'

'Never get between a predator and its prey,' Tom reminded him, as they crept up the mountain.

'Unless we want to be Permian dinner,' Jamie agreed.

There was a wide rocky ledge over the cave, with some dry ferns growing up through a crack in the rock. The boys and Wanna went over to it.

'I reckon it's safe to watch from here,' Tom announced, squatting down on his haunches so he was mostly hidden by the ferns. Jamie and Wanna did the same. Jamie took a second water bottle out of his rucksack and took a long glug.

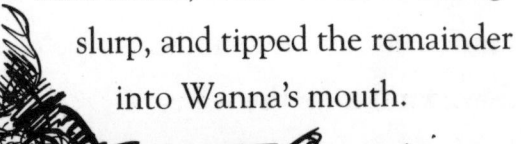

'Finish it off,' he told Tom. 'We'll be going back home, soon.' Tom took a big slurp, and tipped the remainder into Wanna's mouth.

Wanna wagged his tail as he drank.

Jamie's eyes were fixed on the dimeys. They had stopped eating, and were looking up the mountain in their direction.

'Have they spotted us?' he asked nervously.

Before Tom could answer there was an enormous roar. A hairy bear-sized creature was bounding down the mountain! Its two huge sabre-like canine teeth glinted in the sunshine.

Wanna's tail stopped wagging.

'Freeze!' Tom hissed.

The bear-sized creature swept right past the boys' hiding place, so close that the ferns rustled and they could smell the dung-like odour of its mangy red-brown fur.

'It's after the dimeys' dinner.' Tom sighed with relief as the creature leapt onto the cave platform below them.

'But the dimeys aren't going to give it up,' Jamie said. 'Look at their sails!'

The dimetrodons were advancing towards the ferocious monster, fanning out their

spines. Suddenly, they turned sideways to
the predator.

The hairy beast snarled
ferociously at
them.

Before Tom and Jamie's eyes, yellow and black
eye spots popped out along the top edge of

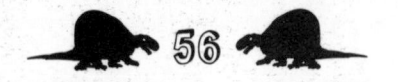

each dimetrodon's sail. There was one between every spine.

Geeowwww!

The dimeys howled.

'Cool!' Jamie and Tom said together.

Wanna gakked in alarm.

The predator paced back and forth, gnashing its sabre-like canine teeth. Now it was moving slower, the boys could see it had powerful shoulders and a thick neck with a broad head and a long scaly reptilian tail.

'It looks like an

enormous hairy rat with no ears,' Tom said. 'We haven't seen a predator with hair before. What is it?'

'I'll find out.' Jamie took the Fossil Finder out of his backpack and flipped it open.

As soon as the words '*HAPPY HUNTING*' appeared, he typed in *PERMIAN PREDATORS*. A grid of pictures popped up.

'It's called inostrancevia.' Jamie carefully read the name and clicked on the picture. 'It was a meat-eating mammal-like reptile that was an ancestor of mammals *and* dinosaurs.'

 58

Garrrr!

The inostie roared.

Geeowww!

The dimeys screeched, rattling the spines
in their sails and stepping sideways towards the
inostie. All at once, they lowered their spines
and raised them. What looked like a battery of
huge eyes belonging to one mega beast flashed
in the sunshine.

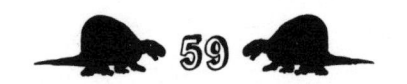

The inostie slunk away, snarling.

'The dimeys scared it off,' Jamie said as the dimeys lowered their sails and continued their disgusting meal. 'So the man in the glasses was right, too.' He packed away the Fossil Finder. 'Now our research is complete. I guess it's time we went back.'

They retraced their steps towards the tunnel that led to the underground cave.

Suddenly, there was a thundering noise behind them. Jamie looked back to see a cloud of red dust. It was coming closer and closer.

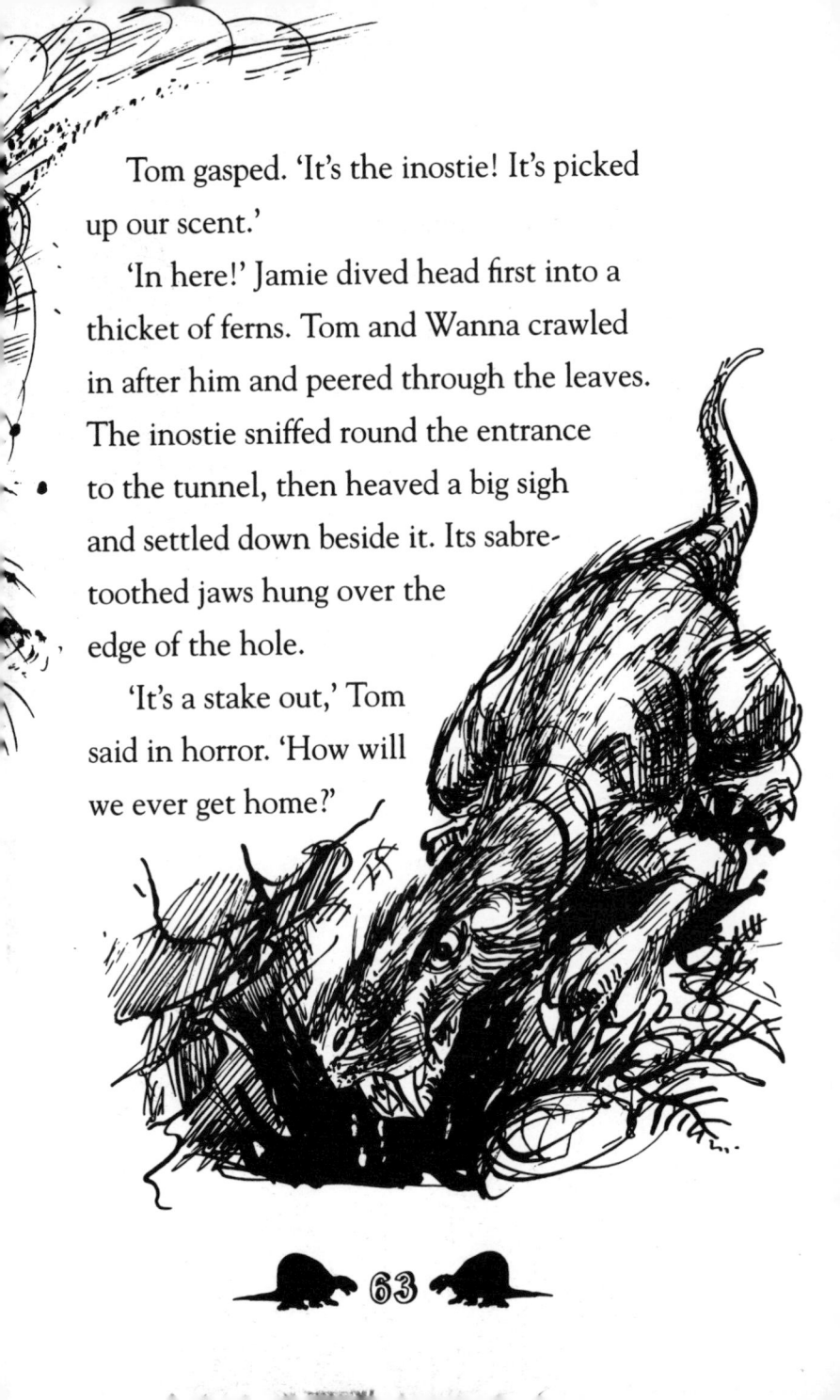

Tom gasped. 'It's the inostie! It's picked up our scent.'

'In here!' Jamie dived head first into a thicket of ferns. Tom and Wanna crawled in after him and peered through the leaves. The inostie sniffed round the entrance to the tunnel, then heaved a big sigh and settled down beside it. Its sabre-toothed jaws hung over the edge of the hole.

'It's a stake out,' Tom said in horror. 'How will we ever get home?'

CHAPTER 6

SEARCH:

ABCDEFGHIJKLM
NOPQRSTUVWXYZ
1234567890 :;.

The inostie's eyes drooped as it lay in wait for its prey to return to the cave entrance. Growl-like snores filled the air.

'It's taking a nap,' Tom whispered, 'but it'll wake up if we try to get down the tunnel.'

'Maybe we can scare it off, like the dimeys did,' Jamie suggested. 'We have to make ourselves look really big and scary. Grab some of those ferns to wave.'

They tugged at the base of the broad-leafed ferns and managed to pull some off. Wanna

stood watching for a moment, then gnawed the top off a small cycad and gripped the rosette of spiky leaves between his jaws.

'They almost look like fangs,' Tom whispered.

'That gives me an idea,' Jamie said. 'If we could get Wanna to stand on our shoulders, we'd look like a huge scary dino.'

'Awesome!' Tom replied.

With Wanna close behind, Jamie and Tom crawled out of the thicket, trying not to rustle the ferns. The inostie snorted in its sleep, but didn't wake up.

'Now for the difficult bit,' Jamie whispered. 'How do you get a dinosaur to stand on your shoulders?'

'By making a pyramid,' Tom said in a low voice. 'Kneel down next to me.' Jamie knelt beside Tom.

'Up, Wanna!' he hissed, holding the ferns in one hand and patting his knee, then his shoulders with the other.

Wanna put his head to one side and blinked, still holding the cycad in his mouth.

'Yeah, we mean it, Wanna. Up!' Tom mirrored Jamie's actions.

Wanna stared at them for what seemed like an age. Then, very slowly, he carefully placed one big foot on Jamie's knee.

'Oof! He weighs a ton.' Tom grimaced as Wanna stepped from Jamie's knee onto their shoulders, turning to face the same direction as the boys.

'Ready?' Jamie asked.

Tom nodded. The boys struggled to their feet, each holding on to one of Wanna's scaly legs. Wanna's toes gripped tighter, and he wobbled a bit, but kept his balance.

'Now screech like dimeys!' Jamie ordered. Geeeooow! Geeow! the boys screeched, waving the giant fern leaves up and down in their free hands.

The inostie's eyes snapped open as it raised its enormous rat-like head. Its beady eyes drilled into them. Drool began to drip from its sabre-like fangs.

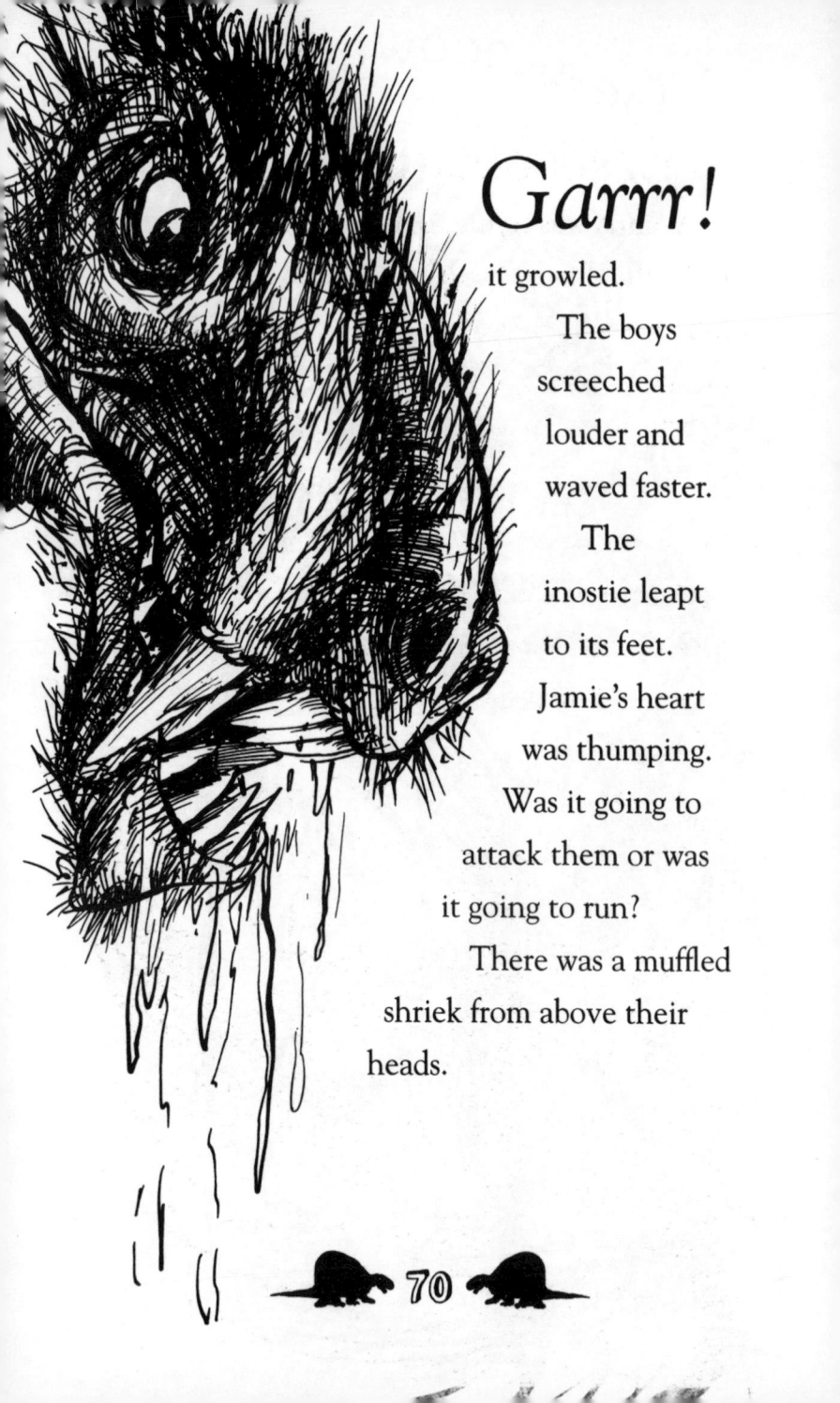

Garrr!

it growled.

The boys screeched louder and waved faster. The inostie leapt to its feet. Jamie's heart was thumping. Was it going to attack them or was it going to run?

There was a muffled shriek from above their heads.

Eeeoooow-unk!

Wanna was trying to imitate the scary noise the dimeys made, with his mouth full of cycad. He was making a hideous racket.

The inostie's eyes opened wide with fear. It put its tail between its legs and ran off into the desert, squealing.

Tom and Jamie dropped the ferns and knelt back down. Wanna spat out the cycad and hopped off their shoulders, grunking wildly.

Eeeoooow-unk!

'We did it!' the boys cheered, springing into the air and giving each other a high five. 'A three-headed Jamie-Tom-Wanna-monster was too much for that big rat. Go, dino team!'

Wanna gambolled happily around them.

'We have to get back,' Jamie said at last. He patted their dino companion on the nose. 'It's time to say goodbye, Wanna.'

'See you next time,' Tom added.

Wanna stood wagging his tail as the boys backed down the tunnel into the

underground cave. There was just enough light
to make out a row of dinosaur footprints in
the sand. First Jamie, then Tom,
stepped backwards into
them, and in another
blinding flash,

the tracks turned to stone beneath their feet, and they were back in the cave in Dinosaur Cove once more. Jamie's dad was in the lighthouse garden, standing next to the table of Permian fossils and talking to the three fossil hunters from before.

'Thanks very much; your trilobite was a great help with our Permian research.' Jamie grinned as he gave the woman with the ponytail back her fossil. 'We found out dimeys could camouflage themselves, like chameleons.'

'I never heard that before,' the woman smiled. 'So, who do you think was right about their sails?' she asked them.

'We reckon dimeys used their sails in all three ways,' Tom told her.

'So all three of you won,' Jamie declared.

'We did!' The adults grinned at each other and stood aside so that the boys could see the fossil table. Their three trilobites were carefully placed on three blue rosettes.

Jamie and Tom looked at Jamie's dad. Mr Morgan shrugged.

'I couldn't choose between them, either,' he laughed.

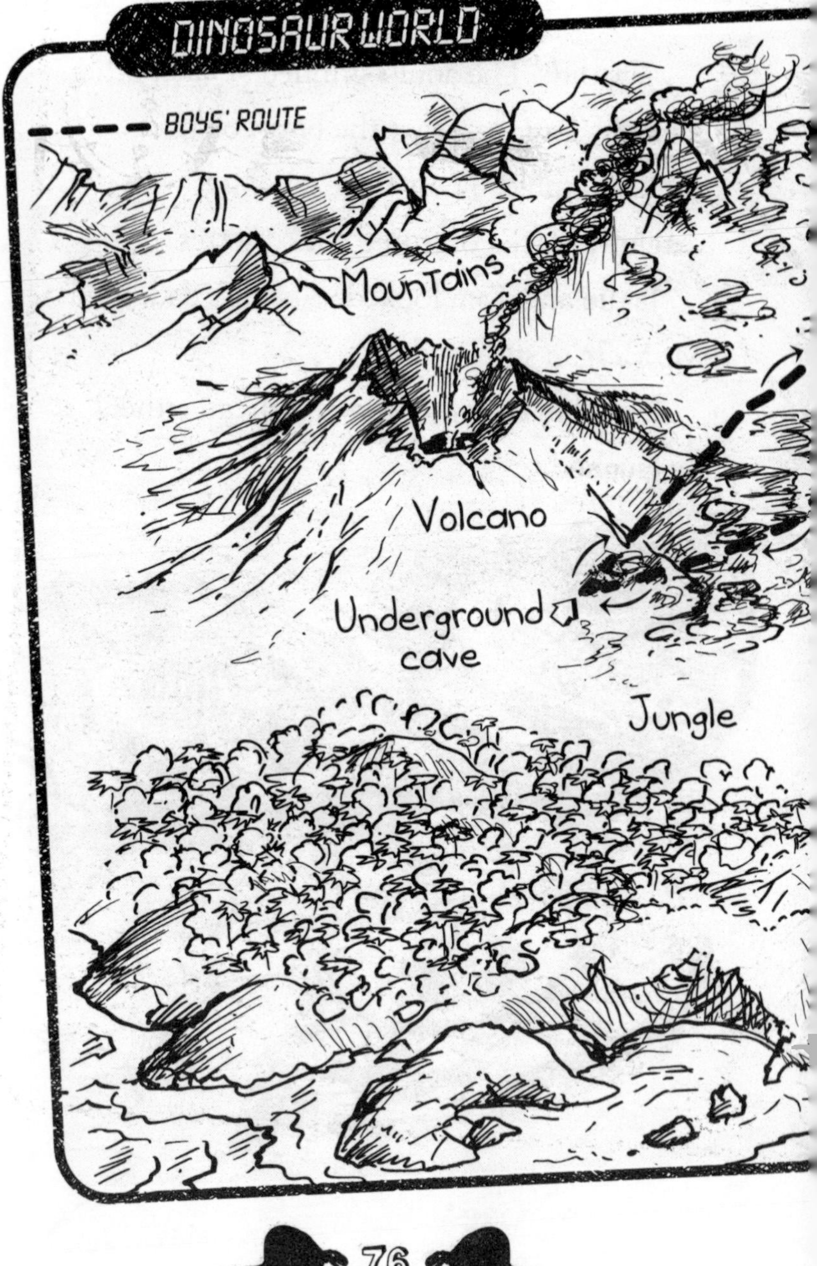
DINOSAUR WORLD
BOYS' ROUTE
Mountains
Volcano
Underground
cave
Jungle

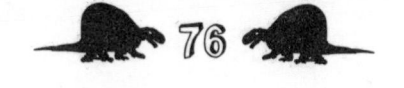

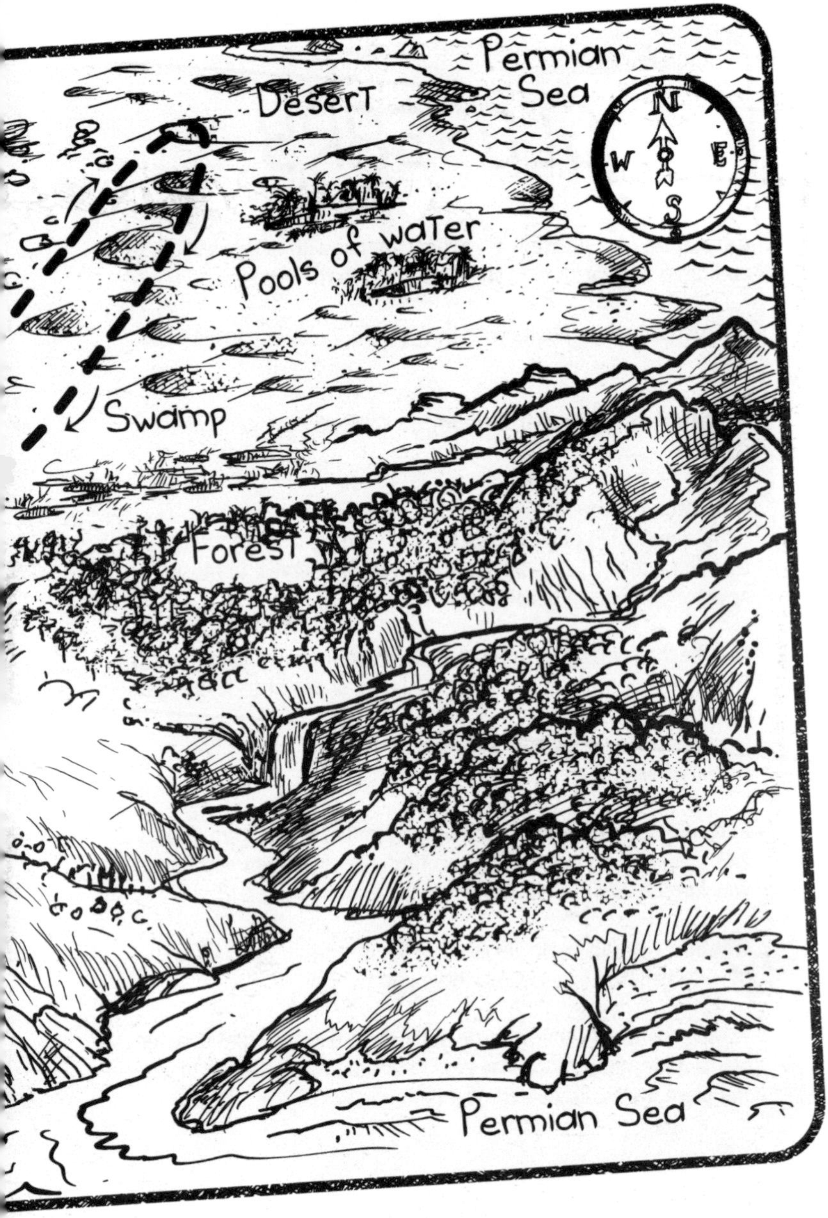
Permian Sea
Desert
N
W
E
S
Pools of water
Swamp
Forest
Permian Sea

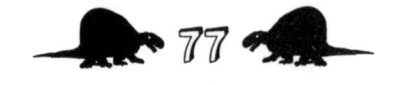

GLOSSARY

Ammonite (am-on-ite) – an extinct animal with octopus-like legs and often a spiral-shaped shell that lived in the ocean.

Cycads (si-kads) – plants with thick trunks, palm-like leaves and cones.

Dimetrodon (dy-mee-tr-oh-don) – a sail-backed, mammal-like reptile.

Extinction event – the Permian era ended with rising temperatures, erupting volcanoes and perhaps even meteors colliding into the Earth. Most species couldn't survive in these new conditions and became extinct.

Fossil – the remains or imprint of plants or animals found in rocks. They help scientists unravel the mysteries of pre-historic times.

Inostrancevia (in-os-tran-see-vee-a) – a large, predatory mammal-like reptile.

Permian (per-mee-an) – the Permian period lasted from 290 to 248 million years ago. During this time the supercontinent Pangaea was formed and non-dinosaur reptiles roamed the earth.

Trilobite (try-loh-byt) – an extinct marine animal that had an outside skeleton divided into three parts.

Wannanosaurus (wah-nan-oh-sor-us) – a dinosaur that only ate plants and used its hard, flat skull to defend itself. Named after the place it was discovered: Wannano in China.